the Pig
who
wished

(Piggy edition)

♥ this book belongs to...

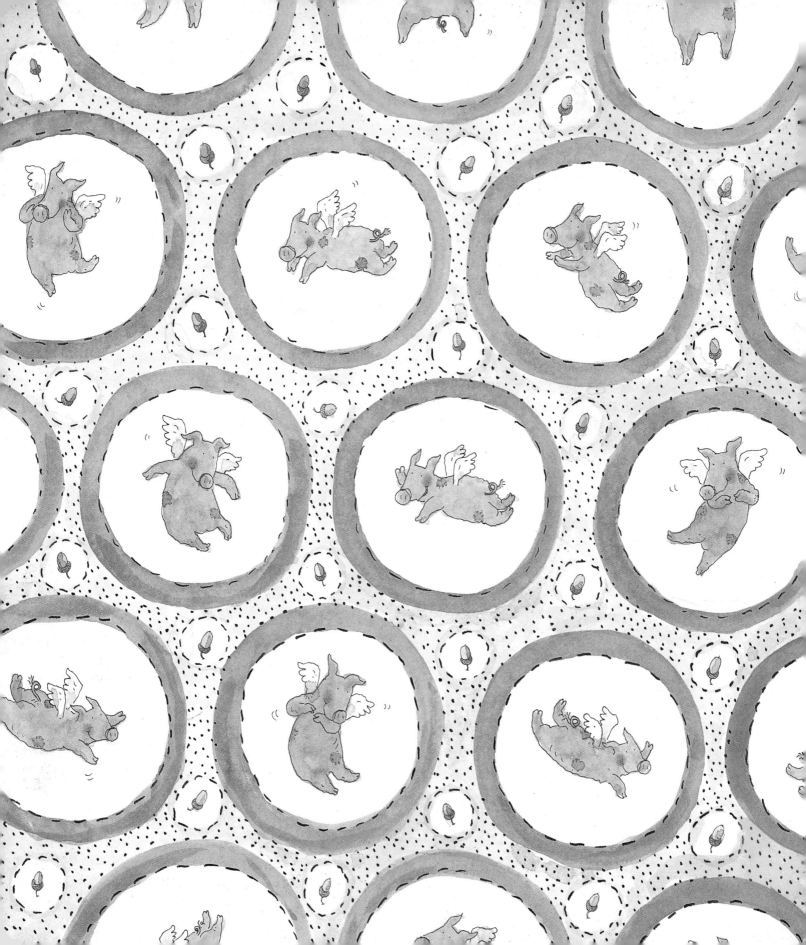

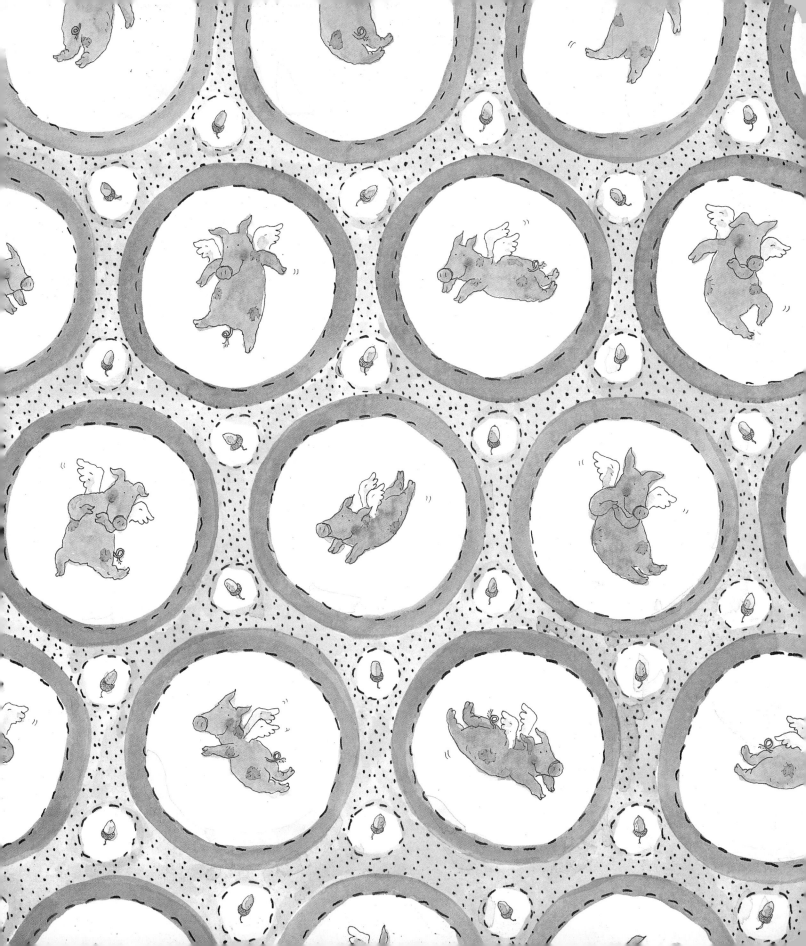

The Pig who Wished

Joyce Dunbar ✿ Illustrated by Selina Young

A Dorling Kindersley Book
First published in Great Britain in 1998
by Dorling Kindersley Limited,
9 Henrietta Street, London WC2E 8PS
Text copyright © 1998 Joyce Dunbar
Illustrations copyright © 1998 Selina Young
The author's and illustrator's moral rights have been asserted.
Visit us on the World Wide Web at
http://www.dk.com

A CIP catalogue record for this book is available from the British Library.
ISBN 0 7513 7154 8 (Hardback)
ISBN 0 7513 7182 3 (Paperback)
Colour reproduction by Dot Gradations, UK
Printed in Hong Kong by Wing King Tong

2 4 6 8 10 9 7 5 3

DORLING KINDERSLEY

Once there was a pig who swallowed a
magic acorn so that all of her wishes came true.
"Oh, I do wish I could get out of my pigpen and
look at the shops," said the pig.

And the pig did get out of her pigpen
and she did look at the shops in the high street.
And nobody minded one bit!

"Oh, I do wish I could go into that teashop and have a pot of tea and a plate of cream buns," said the pig.

And the pig did go into the teashop, and she did have a pot of tea and a plate of cream buns. And nobody minded one bit!

Then a baby went by in a pushchair.

The baby held a cuddly toy pig.

"Oh, I do wish I could ride home with that baby in his pushchair and share all his toys," said the pig.

And the pig did ride home with the baby in his
pushchair and she did share his toys.
And nobody minded one bit!
Then the baby's mummy
said, "Bathtime!"

"Oh, I do wish I could play with that baby in
his bath and make a big Splash!" said the pig.

And the pig did play with the baby in his bath and they did make a big Splash! And nobody minded one bit! Then the baby's daddy came along and said, "Bedtime!"

"Oh, I do wish I could have a piggyback ride with that baby and be tucked up in a warm cosy bed," said the pig.

And the pig did get a piggyback ride with the baby and she was tucked up in a warm cosy bed. And nobody minded one bit!

Then the baby's mummy and daddy said,
"Sleepytime!"

The pig settled down to *try* to sleep but the baby "bounced" around on the bed. So the pig *bounced* around with the baby.

"Oh, I do wish my two little brothers were here, too. We could all bounce around with the baby," said the pig.

And the pig's *two little* brothers were there, too.
And they all bounced around with the baby.
And nobody minded one bit!

"Oh, I do wish that lady from the teashop could come and bounce, too," said the pig.

And the lady from the teashop did come and she bounced on the bed with the baby and the three little pigs. And nobody minded one bit!

"Oh, I do wish that mummy and daddy would join in," said the pig.

And the baby's *mummy* and dadd*y* did join in.
They bounced on the bed with the lady from the
teashop and the baby and *the* t*h*ree little pigs.

BOUNCE!

On to the bed.

The pig was so surprised, she hiccuped. Out of her mouth popped the magic acorn. Her wishes would no longer come true.

Hiccup!

And when the baby's mummy and daddy saw that they had bounced through the floor with the lady from the teashop and the baby and the three little pigs, they did mind. They minded a lot!

"Shoo!"

they shouted at once.

But the baby still didn't mind, not a bit.

Neither did the pig!

for Sarah, Gregory,
and Russell~J.D.

for Georgina and
Angus Darling~S.Y.

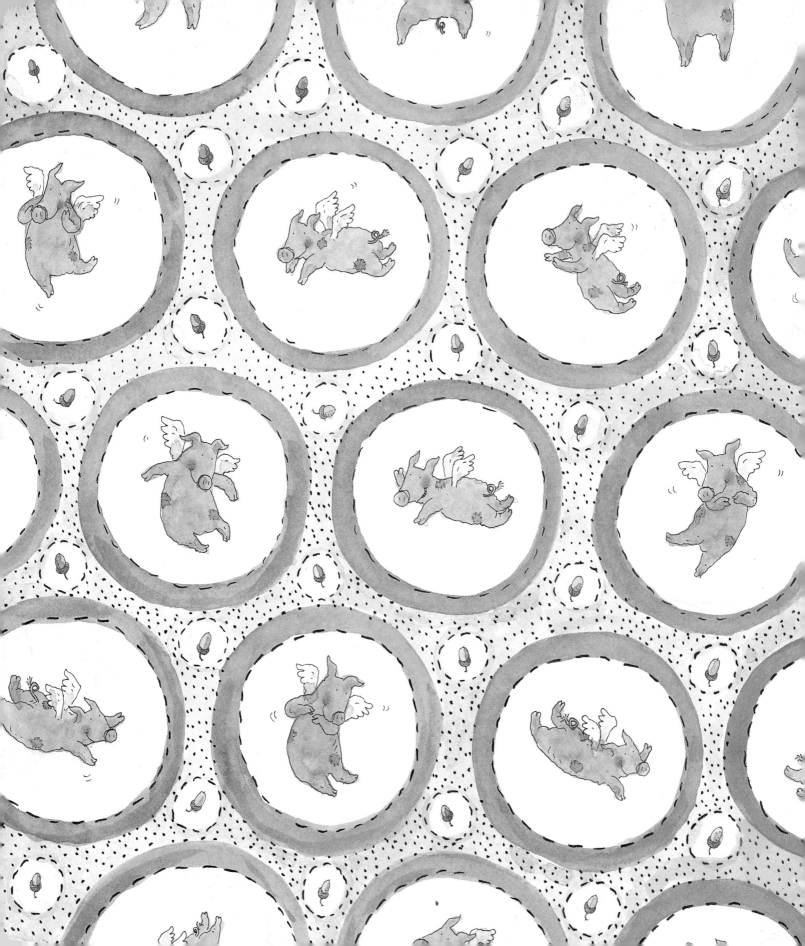

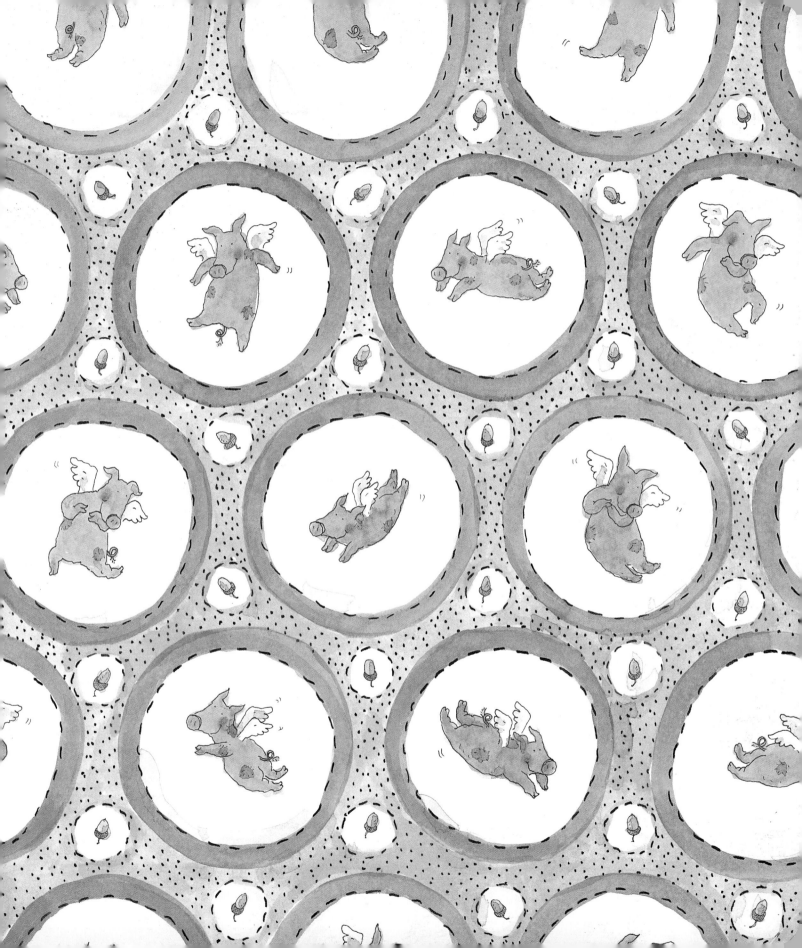

Other Toddler Books to collect -

BABY LOVES by Michael Lawrence, Illustrated by Adrian Reynolds

PANDA BIG AND PANDA SMALL by Jane Cabrera

I'M TOO BUSY by Helen Stephens

CATERPILLAR'S WISH by Mary Murphy